by AMY KROUSE ROSENTHAL and PARIS ROSENTHAL

# Dear Girl,

illustrated by HOLLY HATAM

Dedicated to Sadie and Charlie. xo A.K.R. and P.R.

In memory and celebration of A.K.R.—whose words made this world a brighter and better place —H.H.

HARPER
An Imprint of HarperCollins Publishers

Dear Girl,

Keep that arm raised!
You have smart things to say!

Dear Girl,

Sometimes you may feel like
being pink and sparkly.

Sometimes you may feel
pretty much the opposite.

Dear Girl,

Look at yourself in the mirror.
Say thank you to something
that makes you YOU.

Dear Girl,

Sometimes you just need a good cry.

Sometimes you'll
need a friend.

Sometimes you'll
need to be alone.

Sometimes you'll
need a tissue.

Sometimes you'll need a bucket.

Dear Girl,

Do you know that
there is no such thing as asking
too many questions??

Dear Girl,

Write down your thoughts once in a while,
even if it's just to enjoy the way your pen
feels against the paper.

Dear Girl,

Make your room awesome.

Make your room
*you*.

And while you're at it, make your bed!

*Adventure* is worthwhile in itself.

— Amelia Earhart

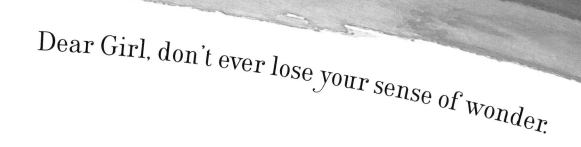

Dear Girl, don't ever lose your sense of wonder.

Dear Girl,

Sometimes you've just gotta stop . . .

AND DANCE!

Dear Girl,

Find people like you.

Find people unlike you.

Dear Girl,

Create traditions,

fun, crazy handshakes,

and silly inside jokes.

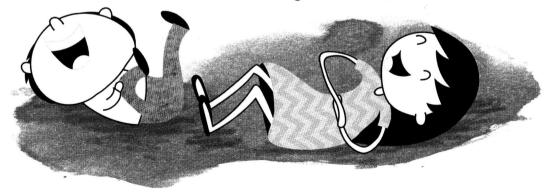

Dear Girl,

If your instinct
is telling you to say no,

say no, you know?

Dear Girl,

Coloring

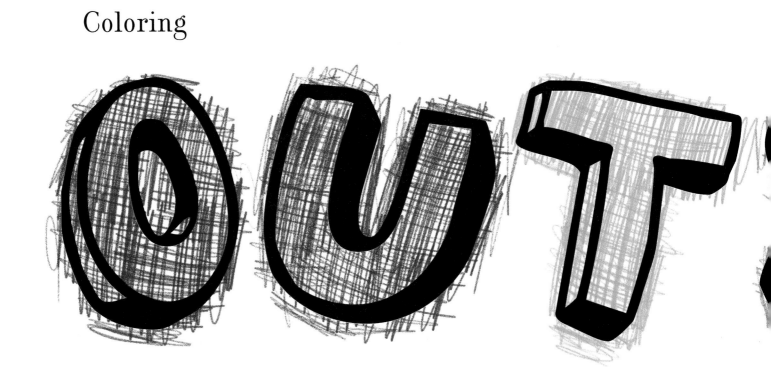

the lines is
cool too.

Dear Girl,

There are no rules about what to wear

or how to cut
your hair.

Dear Girl,

You know what's

really

boring?

When
people
say
how

they are!

Dear Girl,

Listen to your brave side.

Dear Girl,

You won't be invited
to every single party
on the planet.

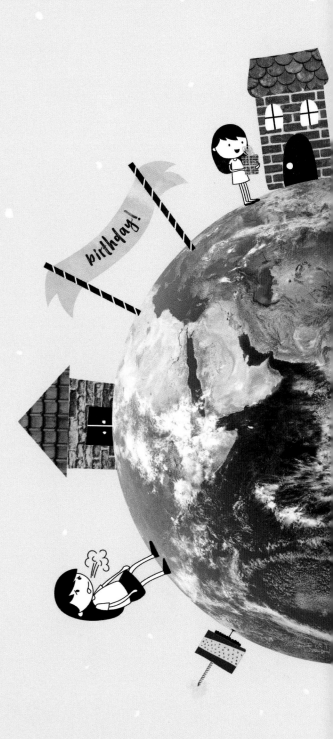

(Which is really okay—
can you imagine how
exhausting that would be?)

Dear Girl,

A tree trunk is the perfect place

for quiet thoughts to be thunk.

Dear Girl,

Whenever you need an
encouraging boost, remember
you can turn to any page in this book.

Most of all, dear girl who I love,
know that you can
always always always . . .

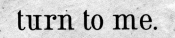

turn to me.